W9-BSC-540

THE COMPLETE
DINOSAUR SCRAPBOOK

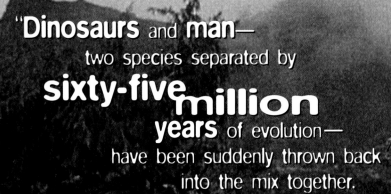

"**Dinosaurs** and **man**—
two species separated by
sixty-five **million**
years of evolution—
have been suddenly thrown back
into the mix together.

How can we have
the **faintest** idea
what to expect?"

—Dr. Alan Grant
Jurassic Park

THE COMPLETE DINOSAUR SCRAPBOOK

by James Preller,
with Molly Jackel and Marilyn McCabe

based on the **Jurassic Park** screenplay
by Michael Crichton and David Koepp, and
The Lost World: Jurassic Park screenplay by David Koepp

based on the novels **Jurassic Park** and
The Lost World by Michael Crichton

SCHOLASTIC INC.

New York   Toronto   London   Auckland   Sydney

To Nickosaurus rex
— J.P.

No part of this publication may be reproduced in whole or in part, or stored in
a retrieval system, or transmitted in any form or by any means, electronic,
mechanical, photocopying, recording, or otherwise, without written permission
of the publisher. For information regarding permission, write to Scholastic Inc.,
555 Broadway, New York, NY 10012.

ISBN 0-590-37399-4

Copyright © 1997 MCA Publishing Rights, a Division of Universal Studios, Inc.
All Rights Reserved. THE LOST WORLD: JURASSIC PARK™ & © 1997 Universal City
Studios, Inc. And Amblin Entertainment, Inc. All Rights Reserved.

TM & © 1997 Universal Studios, Inc. & Amblin Entertainment, Inc. All rights reserved.
JURASSIC PARK and the JURASSIC PARK logo are registered trademarks of
Universal City Studios, Inc. & Amblin Entertainment, Inc. Published by Scholastic Inc.

Book Design: Michael Malone

12 11 10 9 8 7 6 5 4 3   7 8 9/9 0 1 2/0

Printed in the U.S.A.
First Scholastic printing, May 1997

NORTH

SITE B

CK

ISLA MATANCEROS

OCE

ISLA MUERTA

ISLA SORNA

LAS CINCO MUERTES
(THE FIVE DEATHS)

ISLA PENA

ISLA TACANO

CF DF

CK

DE

DD

CJ

DE

DD

It began with a vision.

A solitary spark in one man's imagination. John Hammond saw a world where dinosaurs once again walked the earth. Then he dared to make his dream come true....

ISLA NUBLAR

On a small island 120 miles west of Costa Rica, John Hammond beamed like a proud father. He boasted to his visitors that Jurassic Park was "the most advanced amusement park in the world." He continued, "I'm not talking about just rides. Everybody had rides. We made living biological attractions so astonishing they'll capture the imagination of the entire world!"

And surely, John Hammond was right. For on that small island lived—actually *lived!*—a stunning variety of dinosaur species. Gentle plant eaters and ravenous meat eaters. Dinosaurs with horns and crests, spikes and terrible claws. Dinosaurs with names like Stegosaurus, Gallimimus, Triceratops, Velociraptor, and Tyrannosaurus rex.

The dinosaurs were "controlled" by concrete moats, motion sensor tracking systems, and thirty-foot-high fences—charged with ten thousand volts of electricity. Fifty miles of perimeter fencing ensured the safety of all.

Dr. Ian Malcolm sounded the first warning. "Life will not be contained," he argued. "Life breaks free. It expands to new territories. It crashes through barriers."

Malcolm was right. Life did break free—dangerously, violently, murderously. Those who survived were glad to escape with their lives. Jurassic Park was in ruins.

Yet impossible dreams die hard.

SITE B
ISLA SORNA

Here was something different. Here was an island where dinosaurs thrived beyond the hands of man. No constraining fences, no concrete boundaries. The island provided a complete ecological system where dozens of species lived in social groups. "Isla Nublar was just a showroom," Hammond explained, "something for the tourists. Site B was the factory floor."

Without man's interference, the dinosaurs bred and multiplied. Finally, John Hammond had provided the world with a miraculous gift beyond imagining. Creation. Life itself. Real dinosaurs, living naturally—completely free.

But this time the dinosaurs—once rulers of the land for more than 150 million years—faced a dangerous, new threat: the greed of man.

Greed would win the day.

In the end, life breaks free. Nature claims its rights, without pity or remorse. And a dream—a resplendent, magical dream—was shattered.

John Hammond, for one, had learned something. A lesson, it could be hoped, that others might one day learn. He pleaded to us all, "These creatures require our absence in order to survive, not our help. If we can only step aside, and trust in nature—life will find a way."

How do we know about DINOSAURS ?

Jurassic Park and *The Lost World* are imaginative accounts of what might happen if man could recreate dinosaurs. In fact, we actually know very little about dinosaurs. There are only about two thousand complete skeletons of dinosaurs in the world.

There is an entire branch of science devoted to the study of dinosaurs and the time in which they lived. It's called *paleontology*.

One man named Michael Brett-Surman compared the science of paleontology to being a detective on a murder case. The only problem was that "all the witnesses were dead and all the evidence has been left out in the rain for sixty-five million years."

Yet every year we manage to learn more. Scientists find new evidence, make new guesses, and argue old questions about dinosaur behavior. The quest for knowledge continues. Because it seems that people will always want to know the answer to one, simple question: *What were dinosaurs really like?*

When we first met Dr. Alan Grant and Dr. Ellie Sattler, they were at an archaeological dig. They were unearthing the fossil remains of Velociraptors. Fossils can be actual bones or teeth, spaces left behind in stone where an object lay and decayed, or footprints in the earth.

In *The Lost World*, Sarah Harding was also a paleontologist. She specialized in trying to figure out, from the fossil information, how dinosaurs behaved. For Sarah, visiting Site B at Isla Sorna was a dream come true. Sarah was excited to see the Stegosaurus family because she believed that some baby dinosaurs stayed with their parents after their birth. Now she could prove it.

"There are things
on the island that not only
can kill you,

they want to kill you.

If you take this place lightly,
you'll **never** leave it."

—Dr. Ian Malcolm
The Lost World

THE LOST WORLD
JURASSIC PARK

MEET
THE
CAST

Triceratops

(try•SAIR•a•tops)

As the films showed, dinosaur skin probably was scaly and bumpy. We know this because paleontologists have found fossilized skin impressions.

Imagine what it would be like to actually touch a dinosaur. That's what Dr. Ellie Sattler got to experience in the movie *Jurassic Park*. While on tour of the park, Ellie found a veterinarian nursing a sick Triceratops. Ellie was concerned. She bent down, murmured soothingly, and patted the Triceratops's neck. When Ellie touched the dinosaur, she could feel the wrinkles and bumps of the animal's tough skin.

The average Triceratops stood about eight feet high and was twenty-five feet long.

Those horns were probably just for protection. Triceratops had a huge head—one fossilized skull was seven feet long.

At the end of its nose, Triceratops had a curved beak like a parrot, which might have been used to rip off branches from trees.

In spite of all those frightening horns, Triceratops was a herbivore, or plant eater.

What is a DINOSAUR anyway ?

Dinosaurs were just one of several reptile groups that lived between 225 and 65 million years ago. They had some things in common with other reptiles, but basically dinosaurs were unique in that they were able to walk and run more effectively than other reptiles. Dinosaurs' legs were underneath their bodies rather than coming out the sides of their bodies like, for example, a crocodile's. Also, they were land dwellers— scientists do not include in the dinosaur family any ancient animal that lived in the sea or that flew.

Here's something you may have been able to guess, even without a movie: *Don't mess with an angry Triceratops!* After Roland Tembo, Dieter Stark, and the other hunters had captured many dinosaurs, Sarah Harding and Nick van Owen sneaked into their camp to free the animals. Suddenly free, a confused and frightened Triceratops burst through the side of the tent, causing havoc and destruction as it went. There was only one thing left to do. Get out of the way—*FAST!*

"This guy was my **number one favorite** when I was a kid!"

— Dr. Alan Grant
Jurassic Park

Triceratops were among the last dinosaurs to walk the earth. It is quite possible that the last living dinosaur was a Triceratops.

HEY, I HEARD THAT!
Some scientists call the Triceratops "three-horned face." But not if he's in earshot!

Pachycephalosaurus

(pack•e•SEFF•a•low•SAW•rus)

All was peaceful on Isla Sorna, as herds of dinosaurs quietly grazed. Suddenly, a fleet of pursuit vehicles shattered the calm. Hunters in Jeeps and on motorcycles chased the frightened animals, cutting off individuals for capture.

An exhausted Pachycephalosaurus slowed to a stop, while a hunter raised his rifle. But for a Pachycephalosaurus, the best defense is a good offense. It charged and smashed headfirst right into the side of the Jeep!

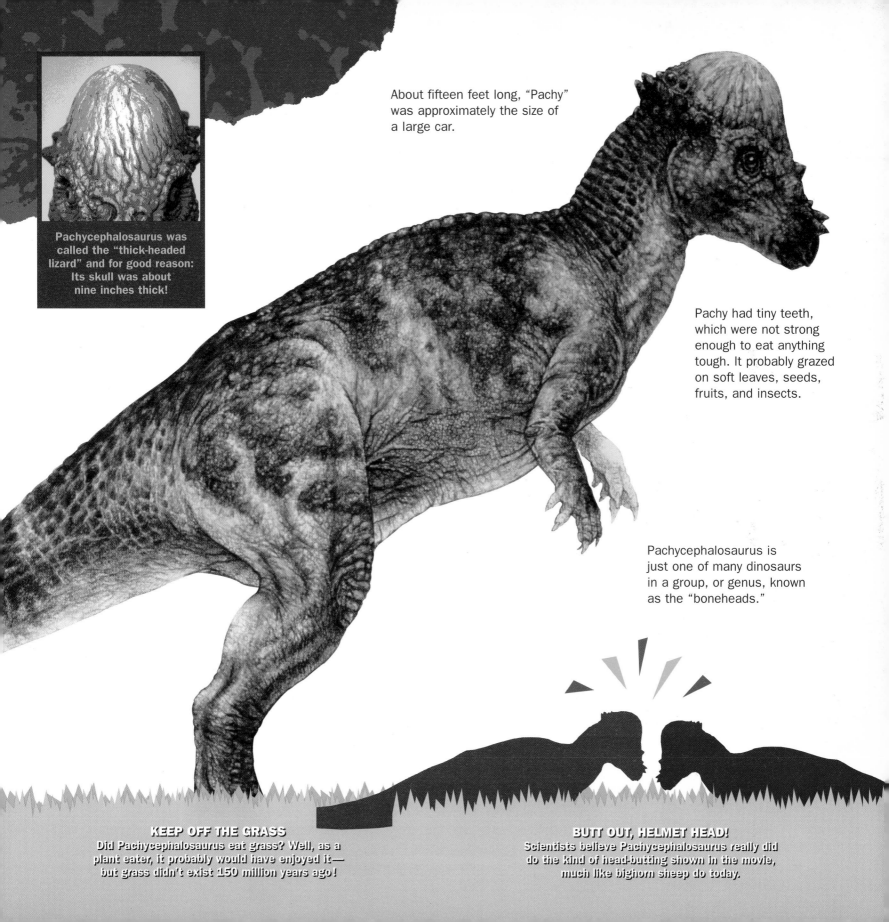

Pachycephalosaurus was called the "thick-headed lizard" and for good reason: Its skull was about nine inches thick!

About fifteen feet long, "Pachy" was approximately the size of a large car.

Pachy had tiny teeth, which were not strong enough to eat anything tough. It probably grazed on soft leaves, seeds, fruits, and insects.

Pachycephalosaurus is just one of many dinosaurs in a group, or genus, known as the "boneheads."

KEEP OFF THE GRASS
Did Pachycephalosaurus eat grass? Well, as a plant eater, it probably would have enjoyed it—but grass didn't exist 150 million years ago!

BUTT OUT, HELMET HEAD!
Scientists believe Pachycephalosaurus really did do the kind of head-butting shown in the movie, much like bighorn sheep do today.

HOW'D THEY DO THAT?

The spectacular roundup scene in *The Lost World* includes many dinosaurs—but not a single model was used. Every dinosaur was created by computer! To film the scene, Industrial Light and Magic (the company that makes the computer-generated dinosaurs) placed bright orange balls on the ground that the Jeeps followed. The balls provided an eyeline for the actors and, more importantly, a path to follow when they digitally inserted the dinosaurs later. A technician walked around with a dinosaur head on a stick for a height reference to show the actors where to look. Also, stunt men and women on horseback led the Jeeps through the field. Then those horses were digitally removed from the scene and replaced with computer-generated dinosaurs!

Stegosaurus
(STEG•o•SAW•rus)

Dr. Ian Malcolm rushed to Isla Sorna to "save" his girlfriend Sarah Harding. But Sarah didn't seem to need rescuing. Malcolm found her happily observing a family of Stegosaurs. She even borrowed Nick van Owen's camera to take a few "family" photos. But when the camera whirred loudly, the biggest Stegosaurus heard the sound and got angry. It turned and lashed its tail at Sarah, who leaped out of the way. Was Sarah scared silly? Not in the least. She threw her arms around Malcolm and exclaimed, "Isn't it great!?"

"Should we
rescue her
now or
after lunch?"

—Nick van Owen
The Lost World

DINO DUMMIES

A Stegosaur's brain was about the size of a walnut, so it's safe to assume that the big fella wasn't thinking Deep Thoughts while munching on all those plants. But today, scientists think that maybe dinosaurs weren't as dim-witted as once believed. Besides, even though Stegosaurs had very small brains, they did manage to survive for 50 million years—and that's not too shabby!

Though the plates look like armor, most experts now believe they were not very useful for defense. One unusual theory, suggested by a Finnish scientist, is that Stegosaurus curled up like a hedgehog when attacked.

Scientists believe the Stegosaurus was probably a slow-moving animal because its rear legs were longer than its front legs. This feature may have allowed Stegosaurus to rear up on its hind legs to get at tall shrubs and leaves on trees.

Two to four pairs of spikes— about three feet long!— stuck out of its tail. The tail spikes were probably the Stegosaur's most effective defense weapon.

Scientists aren't sure about the function of the staggered plates that ran along the back of a Stegosaurus. But most think the plates were used to soak up warmth, like solar panels. And when the animal was too hot, the plates helped Stegosaurus cool down.

Stegosaurus, a plant eater, stood about eleven feet tall and was thirty feet long. Its toes had hooves, and its nose was much like a beak.

MOMMY DEAREST?

In *The Lost World*, there is a lot of debate about how dinosaurs treated their young. While no one can say for certain, recent evidence comes down on the side of Sarah Harding. The fossil record shows that many kinds of dinosaurs did in fact herd together and probably even protected their young.

Tyrannosaurus rex
(tie•RAN•o•SAW•rus REX)

"Our attractions will send kids right **out** of their **minds**." —John Hammond
Jurassic Park

"T-REX DOESN'T WANT TO BE FED, HE WANTS TO HUNT."

—Dr. Alan Grant•*Jurassic Park*

THE CRUEL KING

Tyrannosaurus rex means "tyrant king." A tyrant is a harsh, cruel ruler.

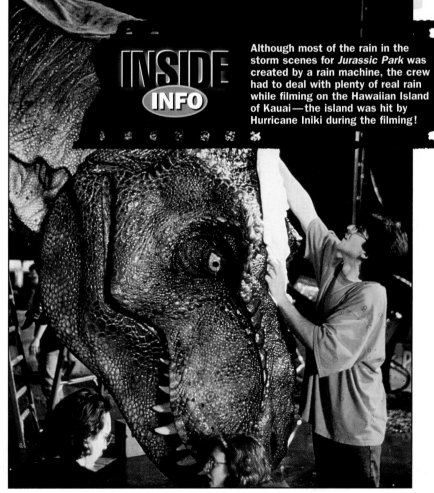

INSIDE INFO

Although most of the rain in the storm scenes for *Jurassic Park* was created by a rain machine, the crew had to deal with plenty of real rain while filming on the Hawaiian Island of Kauai—the island was hit by Hurricane Iniki during the filming!

"Mommy's **very** angry."

—Ian Malcolm
The Lost World

The injured baby T-rex didn't know that Sarah and Nick were trying to mend its broken leg. All it knew was pain, so it cried. Well, there's nothing like the cry of a baby to bring parents running—even if Mom and Dad go by the last name of "rex." When Ian rushed to warn Sarah, it was already too late. Mom and Dad were outside the trailer. And they weren't knocking to borrow a cup of sugar.

"If people had the chance to see **one** dinosaur and one only, **ninety-nine percent** would choose the **Tyrannosaur.**

Now that's **something** to build a theme park around."

—Peter Ludlow
The Lost World

SECONDS anyone ?

Q: What was the first thing the T-rex ate in *Jurassic Park*?

A: A goat

Q: What was the second thing?

A: A tire from a Jeep (frankly, the goat tasted better)

Q: What was the last thing a T-rex ate in *The Lost World*?

A: Peter Ludlow (hey, it was hungry!)

Tyrannosaurus ate an average of about 300 pounds of meat a day. Which means it could chomp down on poor Eddie Carr in *The Lost World*—and still come back for seconds!

Sarah Harding: "How are we going to find the adult?"

Ian Malcolm: "Follow the screams."

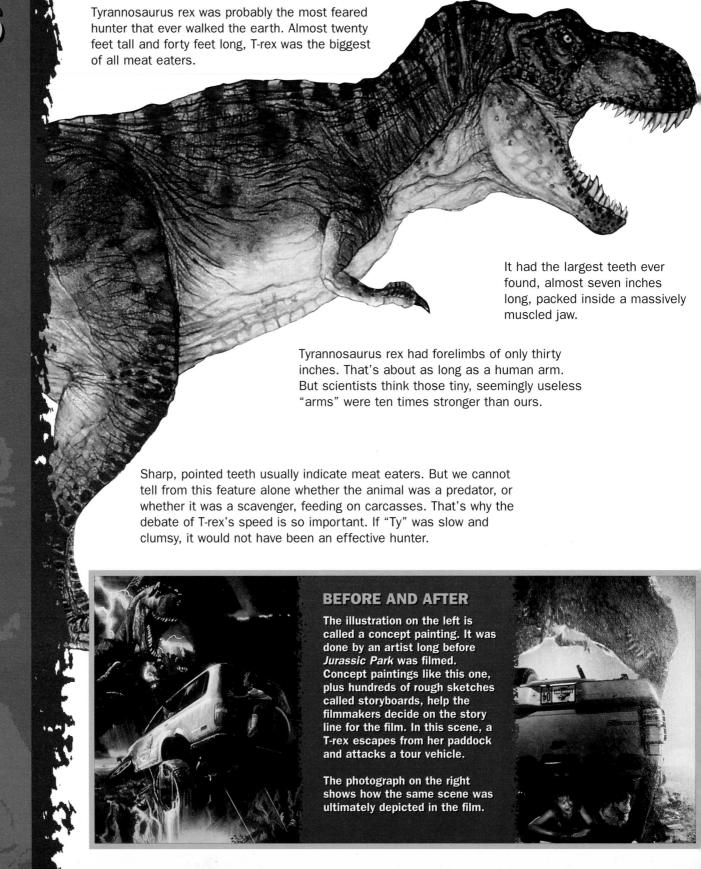

Tyrannosaurus rex was probably the most feared hunter that ever walked the earth. Almost twenty feet tall and forty feet long, T-rex was the biggest of all meat eaters.

It had the largest teeth ever found, almost seven inches long, packed inside a massively muscled jaw.

Tyrannosaurus rex had forelimbs of only thirty inches. That's about as long as a human arm. But scientists think those tiny, seemingly useless "arms" were ten times stronger than ours.

Sharp, pointed teeth usually indicate meat eaters. But we cannot tell from this feature alone whether the animal was a predator, or whether it was a scavenger, feeding on carcasses. That's why the debate of T-rex's speed is so important. If "Ty" was slow and clumsy, it would not have been an effective hunter.

BEFORE AND AFTER

The illustration on the left is called a concept painting. It was done by an artist long before *Jurassic Park* was filmed. Concept paintings like this one, plus hundreds of rough sketches called storyboards, help the filmmakers decide on the story line for the film. In this scene, a T-rex escapes from her paddock and attacks a tour vehicle.

The photograph on the right shows how the same scene was ultimately depicted in the film.

BOOM, BOOM, BOOM. DO RUN RUN!
Roland turned his head to listen for a distant sound: boom. Boom. BOOM. "Did you?" he asked Ian. Both men listened intently. "No," Roland answered himself. "I think we're okay." Ian looked down and saw a puddle rippling in circles. He warned, "No. We're not." Suddenly Tyrannosaurus rex was on the hunt again. And it was time for everybody to run for their lives!

INSIDE INFO

T-rex noises were based on a mix of sounds made by elephants, alligators, penguins, tigers, and dogs, as well as some of the sounds whales make through their blowholes.

After years of debate, most scientists now believe that a Tyrannosaurus could run as fast as thirty miles per hour. Combine that with good sight, a fine sense of smell, and acute hearing, and what have you got?

One mean, lean, eating machine!

I WANT MY MOMMY!
In *The Lost World*, Roland and Ajay found a baby Tyrannosaurus rex still in the nest, eating an animal that its parents probably brought back for it. Did Tyrannosaurus parents really care for their young like this?

Since no T-rex nest has ever been found, scientists have no clear idea of how Tyrannosaurus really dealt with its eggs or its hatchlings. Fossil evidence of other eggs and nests shows that some dinosaurs were born self-sufficient and didn't need any further help from their parents. But other dinosaur babies seemed to stay with the parents for some time. Would T-rex parents have come searching for their baby? We just can't know for sure.

"Somewhere on this island, there exists the greatest predator that ever lived.

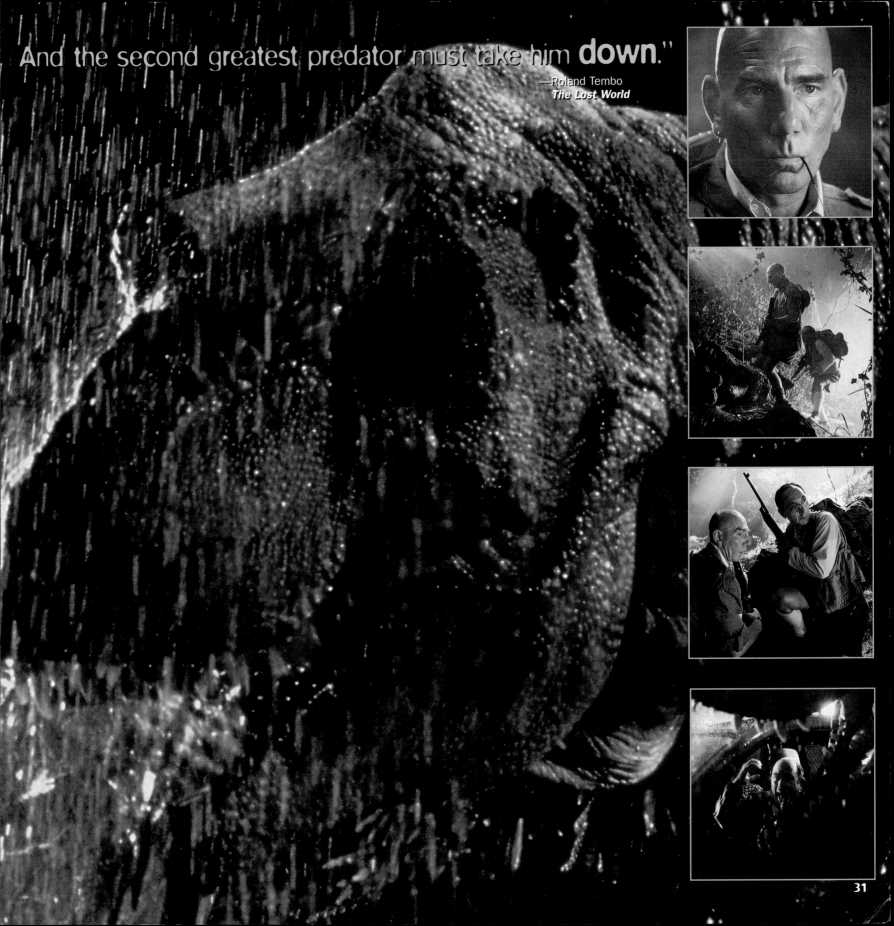

And the second greatest predator must take him **down.**"

—Roland Tembo
The Lost World

Brachiosaurus
(BRA•kee•o•SAW•rus)

INSIDE INFO
The haunting "songs" of the Brachiosaurs were taken from whale songs and an echoed bray of a donkey.

After they had just narrowly avoided becoming snack food for a hungry Tyrannosaurus, Alan, Lex, and Tim came to rest in a large tree. They all fell asleep in the protective arms of the tree limbs. Lex woke up almost nose-to-nose with a Brachiosaurus, a gentle herbivore—"A veggie-saurus, Lex," Tim explained. After calming down (Lex wasn't too keen about dinosaurs, particularly after meeting old T-rex), Lex tried to make friends. She held out a leafy branch for the Brachiosaurus. But she should have been holding a handkerchief. The big guy sneezed all over her. Gross!

Brachiosaurus was like a huge, fat giraffe—about seventy-five feet long and forty feet tall.

SOUND BITE

Tim Murphy:
"What do you call a blind dinosaur?"

Alan Grant:
"What?"

Tim Murphy:
"A Do-you-think-he-saurus. What do you call a blind dinosaur's dog?"

Alan Grant:
"You got me."

Tim Murphy:
"A Do-you-think-he-saurus rex."

THE HOLE STORY

One puzzling feature of Brachiosaurus is that they had holes centered above their eyes. The holes might have been nostrils, or possibly a sort of cooling vent to help keep the huge animal from getting overheated.

Brachiosaurus moved its head and neck from side-to-side, up as high as a four-story building, and down to the ground, probably eating all the leaves and ferns in sight.

Brachiosaurus weighed as much as twelve African elephants and needed to eat about four hundred pounds of food a day.

Compsognathus

(KOMP•so•NAY•thus)

Ah, what a pretty place for a picnic. So young Cathy Bowman decided to have a look around. Suddenly, a small, birdlike creature hopped out from the bushes. Charmed, Cathy lured it toward her with a piece of sandwich. But in an instant, she was surrounded by dozens of darting, bobbing little dinosaurs. "Wh-what do you guys want?" Cathy asked, growing nervous. She was out of food. But alas, those cute, "harmless" creatures were still hungry.

One of the smallest dinosaurs, Compsognathus was birdlike in its body and about the size of a chicken. But don't let looks fool you, this little guy could do some major damage.

The Compsognathus was a carnivore with very sharp teeth, a narrow head, long legs, and a long tail. It had short arms with two toes, much like a miniature version of Tyrannosaurus rex.

"Mom! Dad! You gotta come see this! I found something!"

—Cathy Bowman, island visitor
The Lost World

Compsognathus must have been a swift and efficient hunter. Scientists believe that Compys caught and ate small reptiles with their hands.

EUREKA!

Some say that the connection between birds and dinosaurs was made by dinosaur specialist T. H. Huxley in the late 1800's. He got the idea as he was carving turkey on Christmas Day. While cutting the drumstick, Huxley noticed how similar it was to the dinosaur fossils he had seen.

LAST MEAL

In Germany, a complete skeleton of Compsognathus was discovered—along with the skeleton of a small lizard inside Compy's stomach cavity!

HUNTING IN PACKS

Although scientists are not sure about Compsognathus, they believe that some dinosaurs did hunt in packs. The smaller hunters would outnumber and overwhelm the larger prey—just like in the movie.

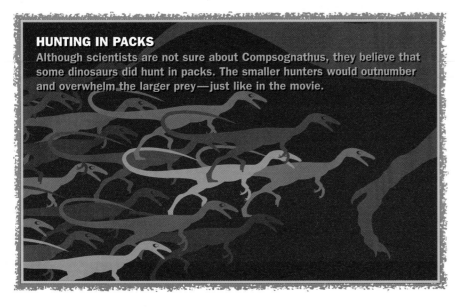

What would happen if man and dinosaur once again shared the earth? If greedy guys like Peter Ludlow had their way, dinosaurs would become "product assets" without rights— hunted, captured, locked in a cage, and sold for profit.

"It gives me the **creeps.** It's like it's **not scared.**"

—Dieter Stark
The Lost World

Its name means "elegant jaw," because of its delicate head and jaws.

INSIDE INFO

In *The Lost World*, all the scenes with Compsognathus were done with remote control robots. To create the effect of pecking and biting, small pieces of Velcro were attached to their mouths and to the actor they were biting. By moving the Velcro all over the person, it looked as if the Compy was on a vicious attack!

Dilophosaurus

(die•LOAF•o•SAW•rus)

"Uh—nice boy. Nice boy. Okay. Run along."

—Dennis Nedry
Jurassic Park

Dilophosaurus was thought to be about twenty feet long (much bigger than the film version). It was an agile carnivore, or meat eater, with long teeth and sharp claws.

NO-FRILLS DINOSAUR

No one really knows whether or not the Dilophosaurus had those fancy, colorful frills around its neck. But maybe the creators of the movie got the idea from the Australian frilled lizard.

Dilophosaurus did have a funny crest on its head—two bony ridges that stuck up like semicircles—but the cobralike fan that expanded and quivered just before it attacked Nedry was entirely the idea of the movie's creators.

Scientists disagree about whether Dilophosaurus chased and attacked its prey, or whether it was a scavenger like a vulture, eating animals that were already dead.

39

In *Jurassic Park*, Dennis Nedry was racing to get the stolen dinosaur embryos off the island. But during the storm, he had trouble with his Jeep. Then he had even more trouble with a Dilophosaurus. "Go fetch," Nedry said, throwing a stick off to the side. The curious Dilophosaurus only hooted and hopped closer. Nedry muttered, "No wonder you're extinct. I'm gonna run you over when I come back down." Big mistake. The Dilophosaurus flared his hood and spit a huge black glob of poison goo into Nedry's eyes. Nedry scrambled back to the Jeep, slammed the door, and thought he was safe. But suddenly the Dilophosaurus appeared on the passenger side—and Dennis Nedry had taken his last ride.

SPITSVILLE
There is no way to know whether any dinosaur actually spat gobs of venom at its prey. Yet it is certainly possible. Besides, what a cool and gross idea!

INSIDE INFO

The Dilophosaurus that attacked Nedry was a full body puppet with interchangeable heads. The Dilo's sounds were taken from the calls of an egret, a large white marsh bird, and swans.

(par•a•SAW•OL•a•fus)

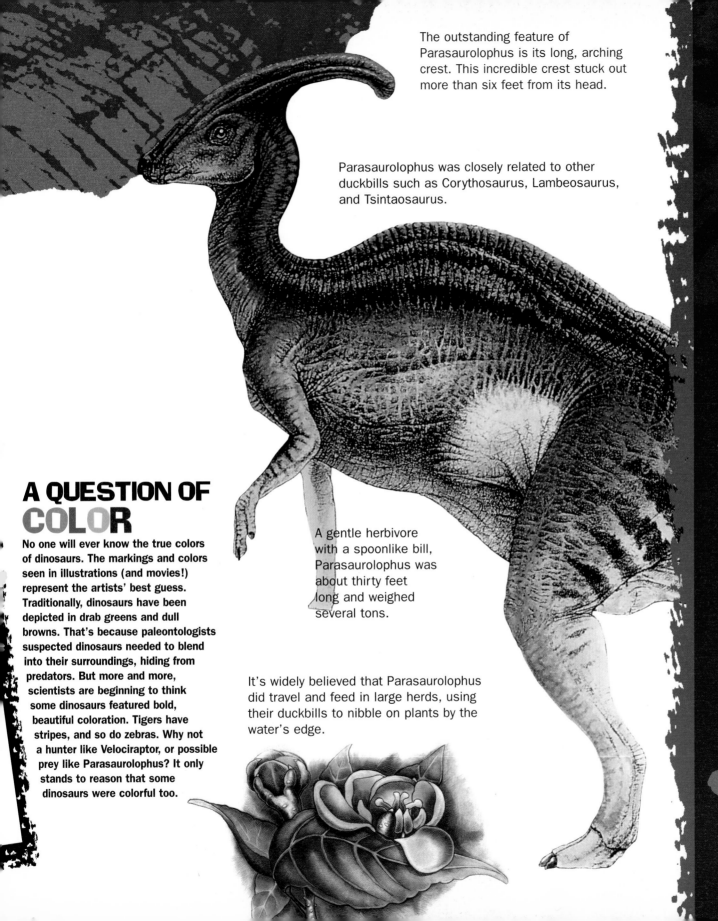

The outstanding feature of Parasaurolophus is its long, arching crest. This incredible crest stuck out more than six feet from its head.

Parasaurolophus was closely related to other duckbills such as Corythosaurus, Lambeosaurus, and Tsintaosaurus.

A QUESTION OF COLOR

No one will ever know the true colors of dinosaurs. The markings and colors seen in illustrations (and movies!) represent the artists' best guess. Traditionally, dinosaurs have been depicted in drab greens and dull browns. That's because paleontologists suspected dinosaurs needed to blend into their surroundings, hiding from predators. But more and more, scientists are beginning to think some dinosaurs featured bold, beautiful coloration. Tigers have stripes, and so do zebras. Why not a hunter like Velociraptor, or possible prey like Parasaurolophus? It only stands to reason that some dinosaurs were colorful too.

A gentle herbivore with a spoonlike bill, Parasaurolophus was about thirty feet long and weighed several tons.

It's widely believed that Parasaurolophus did travel and feed in large herds, using their duckbills to nibble on plants by the water's edge.

COOL CREST

It is believed that Parasaurolophus could make trumpeting sounds by forcing air from its mouth up into its hollow crest, then out through its snout. This noise would have been a useful way of communicating danger or, perhaps, bellowing a challenge to a rival.

WET THEORY

Scientists once thought Parasaurolophus used its long crest like a snorkel to breath underwater. But that theory was all wet—the crest, though hollow, didn't have holes at the top end!

Velociraptor
(vel•AH•si•rapt•or)

"The Raptor is contained in the shed?" asked Grant. "Yeah," Ellie answered, "unless they've learned how to turn doorknobs." Click. *Never underestimate the intelligence of a Raptor.* As Tim and Lex watched in horror from their hiding places in the kitchen, the door handle slowly turned. The door opened and the Raptor looked in. In an instant the Raptor was inside, with a second one close behind. And the hunt was on.

"The Raptor fences aren't out, **are they?**"

—Robert Muldoon
Jurassic Park

Some scientists think Velociraptor may have been striped, like a tiger.

Velociraptor, the "swift thief," was thought to be about six feet long. Although it was relatively small, Velociraptor was very well-equipped for its carnivorous lifestyle.

Velociraptors were probably swift, agile runners. Scientists believe they may indeed have traveled in packs, working together to bring down larger prey. They had large brains and large eyes, and may have had keen senses much like today's birds.

It had large fangs, sharp claws on its three-fingered forelimbs, strong arms, and a particularly long claw on the second toe of each foot. That long claw may have been retractable, like a cat's claws.

"They gave up. They're not chasing us."

—Unknown hunter
The Lost World

The hunters breathed sighs of relief as they looked back. The Tyrannosaurus hadn't followed them into the high grass. But the danger wasn't over, not by a long shot. In the blink of an eye, one man was down. Then another. And as Ajay looked around him, he realized that his worst fear had come to pass. He was surrounded by Raptors. Really, what *could* he do—but close his eyes and wait for the end.

INSIDE INFO

Sometimes the Velociraptors were actually humans in a Velociraptor suit. There was also a full-size mechanical puppet used, and three separate heads for head shots. The newborn baby Raptor breaking out of its shell was actually a mechanical puppet.

Sound BITE

John Hammond:
"This is a delay, that's all this is. All major theme parks have had delays. In 1956, when Disneyland opened, nothing worked."

Ian Malcolm:
"Yes, John. But if the Pirates of the Caribbean breaks down, the pirates don't eat the tourists."

An Educated Guess

How do scientists know how fast a dinosaur ran? They don't! But by comparing the distance between a dinosaur's footprints to the height of its leg, scientists can *estimate* its running speed.

A Feathered Fiend

Because of its close ancestry with birds, some scientists have depicted Velociraptor with feathers.

"They don't try to **bite the jugular,** like a lion, they just slash here, here— or maybe across the belly...

Point is, you're **alive** when they start to **eat** you."

—Dr. Alan Grant
Jurassic Park

Here's a list of some of the characters who are attacked by dinosaurs in both Jurassic Park movies:

DENNIS NEDRY

He made a hearty snack for a Dilophosaurus. The moral: Never pick up hitchhikers.

DONALD GENNARO

Rex trapped him in an outhouse. When you gotta go, you gotta go!

RAY ARNOLD

He thought he'd give Ellie a hand. Instead he gave her an arm. Yuck!

ROBERT MULDOON

The hunter became the hunted... but saved Ellie in the process.

CATHY BOWMAN

She was the girl on the island at the beginning of *The Lost World*. The Compys didn't kill her, but they sure ruined her vacation.

EDDIE CARR

He died saving the lives of Nick, Sarah, and Ian.

DIETER STARK

You could say this meanie got his just desserts. Or maybe just that the Compys got their dessert—Dieter!

DR. BURKE

Nowhere to run, nowhere to hide.

AJAY SIDHU

He nobly tried to save the others, but he could not save himself.

CARTER

He was Dieter's driver. Carter didn't actually get eaten...just stepped on! Splat!

Humanosaurus

(HYU•man•o•SAW•rus)

The following creatures—some peaceful, some fierce—can be found in the films *Jurassic Park* and *The Lost World*. Several are in both! Note: While dinosaurs ruled the land for more than 150 million years, humans have been around for only two million years.

FIRST SEEN IN *JURASSIC PARK*

❶ John Hammond

"Spared no expense" was Hammond's motto. It was his dream—and money—that made Jurassic Park possible.

CLASSIC LINE: "Creation is an act of sheer will."

FROM *THE LOST WORLD*: "These creatures require our absence in order to survive, not our help."

② Dr. Ian Malcolm
The fast-talking "chaotician" who feared the worst about Jurassic Park. A chaotician is a mathematician who believes that disorder rules the universe.

CLASSIC LINE: "Boy, do I hate being right all the time."
FROM *THE LOST WORLD*: "Yeah, *oooh*, *aaah*, that's how it always starts. Screaming and running comes later."

③ Dr. Alan Grant
Happiest digging around for old bones, Grant believed dinosaurs had more in common with present-day birds than reptiles.

CLASSIC LINE: "By the way, Mr. Hammond. After careful consideration, I've decided not to endorse Jurassic Park."

④ Dr. Ellie Sattler
A dedicated paleobotanist who came to inspect Jurassic Park—even if it meant sticking her hand deep into a mound of dino droppings.

CLASSIC LINE (spoken to Hammond):
"People are dying, John."
SECOND BEST: "Dinosaurs eat man. Women inherit the earth."

⑤ Tim Murphy
Hammond's nine-year-old grandson. Tim loved dinosaurs, but he wasn't too crazy about heights.

CLASSIC LINE (at the first tremor of an approaching Tyrannosaurus): "Did you feel that?"

⑥ Alexis (Lex) Murphy
Hammond's granddaughter. Lex loved computers—and her hacker ability helped save lives.

CLASSIC LINE: "Timmy is a dinosaur. A jerkosaurus."

⑦ Robert Muldoon
Game warden for the park, Muldoon was probably the one man who knew just how dangerous the Raptors really were.

CLASSIC LINE (about the Raptors):
"They should all be destroyed."

⑧ Dennis Nedry
The primary architect of the park's computer systems. Also: a dirty, double-crossing thief who got exactly what he deserved.

CLASSIC LINE: "I finished debugging the phones, but the system's compiling for eighteen minutes. One or two minor systems may switch on and off."

⑨ Ray Arnold
A control room technician who inherited the mess that Nedry left behind.

CLASSIC LINE (also his last): "Three minutes and I'll have the power back on in the entire park."

⑩ Donald Gennaro
A lawyer for John Hammond, Gennaro thought Jurassic Park would make him fabulously rich.

CLASSIC LINE: "We are going to make a fortune with this place. A fortune."

MALCOLM'S principles

Here's a recap of Dr. Malcolm's favorite theories:

The Heisenberg Uncertainty Principle:

"Whatever you study, you also change."

Gambler's Ruin:

"A statistical phenomenon.

Says everything in the world

goes in streaks. It's real, you see it

everywhere—in baseball, in blackjack,

in stock markets. Once things go

bad, they tend to stay bad.

Bad things cluster."

The Butterfly Effect:

"A butterfly can flap its wings in

Peking and in Central Park you get rain

instead of sunshine."

Chaos Theory:

While waiting for the Tyrannosaurus

to eat the goat, Malcolm notes,

"You see? The Tyrannosaurus obeys

no set patterns or park schedules.

It's the essence of Chaos."

"The RAPTORS are my favorite. They move so smooth and cool."

Actress Vanessa Lee Chester, who plays twelve-year-old Kelly Malcolm in *The Lost World*, had this to say about working with dinosaurs:

"It was so much fun, it was so cool just seeing the dinosaurs work. The freaky thing was that they were SO real—they would breathe and their veins would bulge and they'd snort! The dinosaurs had this slop on their tongues. We would touch it and scream *Ewwww!* It was really slimy and gross."

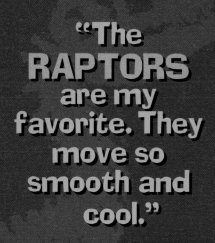

FIRST SEEN IN *THE LOST WORLD*

❶ Dr. Sarah Harding
A fearless paleontologist who specialized in behavioral study. She went to Site B to study dinosaurs in their "natural" habitat.

CLASSIC LINE: "I waited a lifetime for this opportunity. I won't let them take it away."

❷ Nick van Owen
He came to Isla Sorna with Ian Malcolm and Eddie Carr to rescue Sarah Harding—and to make life difficult for Peter Ludlow and friends.

CLASSIC LINE (spoken to Tembo): "What's the matter with you? This animal exists on the planet for the first time in tens of millions of years, and the only way you can express yourself is to kill it?"

❸ Eddie Carr
A field equipment specialist who never really understood what he was in for when he agreed to help John Hammond.

CLASSIC LINE (also his last, spoken with great conviction): "Aaaarrrgghh!"

❹ Dr. Robert Burke
A dinosaur expert brought in by Ludlow. In Burke's view, the Tyrannosaurus rex was a ravenous hunter, not a nurturing parent.

CLASSIC LINE (also his last): "Get out of the way!"

❺ Roland Tembo
A big-game hunter who was bored by the hunt—until Ludlow presented him with the greatest challenge of all.

CLASSIC LINE: "I have spent enough time in the company of death."

❻ Dieter Stark
A hunter who was second in command under Tembo. Stark displayed little respect for the animals he hunted.

CLASSIC LINE: "I'm certain we can handle ourselves against anything."

❼ Ajay Sidhu
Tembo's friend and his most reliable, experienced tracker. A veteran of many big-game expeditions.

CLASSIC LINE (also his last): "NO! Don't go into the long grass!"

❽ Kelly Malcolm
Malcolm's twelve-year-old daughter. She disobeyed her father and sneaked onto Isla Sorna. Big mistake.

CLASSIC LINE (which she *really* should have thought of earlier): "I don't want to be here, I want to be somewhere safe, I want to be somewhere else."

❾ Peter Ludlow
He took over InGen Corporation from his uncle, John Hammond. Ludlow dreamed of making millions by building a dinosaur zoo in San Diego, California.

CLASSIC LINE: "An extinct animal that's brought back to life has no rights. It exists because we made it. We own it."

"I'm sick
of scratching around
in rock and bone
and making guesses
about the nurturing habits
of animals
that have been
dead
for sixty-five
million
years."

— Sarah Harding
The Lost World

THE

SCIENCE OF

JURASSIC

PARK

Why is it called "Jurassic Park"?

Paleontologists divide the history of the earth into four main sections. The earliest is called Precambrian Time. At this stage in the earth's development, life was thought to exist only in the sea. Next came the Paleozoic Era, which saw the development of plant life both in the sea and on land, and the early beginnings of animals. The Mesozoic or "middle life" Era was the time of dinosaurs and the ancestors of all animals still living today. We are currently in the Cenozoic Era, or the age of "recent life."

TRIASSIC PERIOD

245 to 208 million years ago

Scientists believe there was just one huge continent and one huge sea, and the climate was very dry. Conifer trees (evergreen trees with long needles), palmlike trees, and ferns grew in moister areas. There were no flowering plants. Reptiles were the dominant life-form on land, and some small flying reptiles existed. Toward the end of the Triassic Period, early dinosaurs developed, such as Plateosaurus and Coelophysis.

> The Mesozoic Era is divided into three parts, called periods: Triassic, Jurassic, and Cretaceous.

JURASSIC PERIOD

208 to 146 million years ago

The climate got cooler and damper. There were more plants growing in a greater variety of areas. More animals existed—on land, in the sea, and in the air. The single continent that existed in the Triassic Period began to break apart, and volcanic activity was forming new land. Many varieties of dinosaurs and reptiles existed. Flying reptiles were becoming more birdlike. Sea creatures were evolving with fins and flippers. Common dinosaurs of this period include: Camptosaurus, Stegosaurus, Diplodocus, Brachiosaurus, and Allosaurus.

Stegosaurus · Baby T-rex · Baby Stegosaurus · Adult Triceratops · Baby Triceratops

18' · 15' · 12' · 9' · 6' · 3'

PRECAMBRIAN TIME   **PALEOZOIC ERA**

	CAMBRIAN	ORDOVICIAN	SILURIAN	DEVONIAN	CARBONIFEROUS
4-5 billion years ago	570 million years ago	500 million years ago	435 million years ago	400 million years ago	350 million years ago

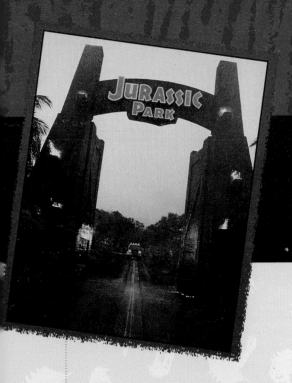

CRETACEOUS
PERIOD
146 to 65 million years ago

This was a period of great change. The continents continued to break apart, seasons became more changeable, and even more plants and animals evolved. By the late Cretaceous Period, many of the trees we know today, like oaks and maples, began to evolve. Flowering plants first appeared. Life-forms varied from small bees to dinosaurs such as Tyrannosaurus, Triceratops, Pachycephalosaurus, and Parasaurolophus. The end of the dinosaurs—and many, many other forms of life—occurred as this period came to a close.

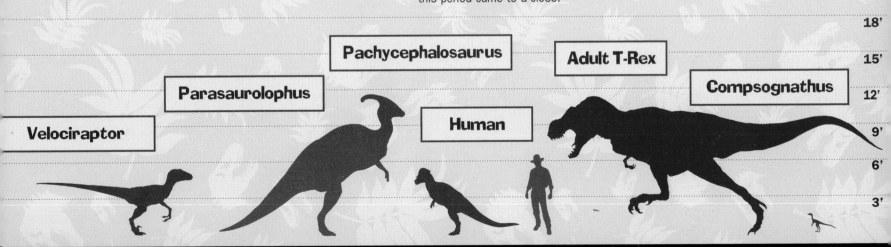

Pachycephalosaurus

Parasaurolophus

Adult T-Rex

Compsognathus

Velociraptor

Human

18'
15'
12'
9'
6'
3'

MESOZOIC ERA				CENOZOIC ERA	
PERMIAN 290 million years ago	**TRIASSIC** 225 million years ago	**JURASSIC** 180 million years ago	**CRETACEOUS** 135 million years ago	**TERTIARY** 70 million years ago	**QUATERNARY** 2 million years ago–present

What's in a name?

Names for dinosaurs—like most scientific names—are usually taken from Latin or ancient Greek. For example: *Ceratops* means horned face. *Tri* means three. **Triceratops**: a three-horned face! Names may also come from places, people, or behavior. For instance: *Veloci* means swift. *Raptor* means thief. **Velociraptor**: The swift thief!

PART OF NAME	ORIGIN	MEANING
Brachio	Greek	Arm
Cephalic	Greek	Head
Ceratops	Greek	Horned face
Compso	Greek	Elegant
Cory	Greek	Helmet
Dactyl	Greek	Finger, toe
Di	Greek	Two
Dino	Greek	Terrible
Lopho	Latin	Ridged
Lophus	Latin	Crested
Mimus	Latin	Imitator
Odon	Greek	Tooth
Pachy	Greek	Thick
Raptor	Latin	Thief
Saurus	Greek	Lizard
Stego	Greek	Roof
Tri	Greek	Three
Tyranno	Greek	Tyrant
Veloci	Latin	Swift

Sometimes dinosaurs got their names from the person who first discovered the fossils. For example, there's even a dinosaur known as "Albertosaurus!" Poor thing, the other dinosaurs must have had a hard time taking him seriously.

A "Saltasaurus" didn't get its name based on behavior—no one knows if it liked salt. Actually, it's because its skeleton remains were found in Salta, Argentina.

Paleontology means "the science of ancient beings." And no, wise guy, that doesn't include your parents!

Could we really make dinosaurs come to life again?

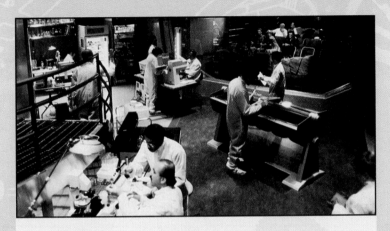

Scientists in the *Jurassic Park* movie used the blood from a mosquito frozen in amber to "clone" dinosaurs. A "clone" (from the Greek word meaning "twin") is an exact copy of a living thing, with exactly the same genetic material. This material, known as DNA—the building blocks of life—contains all the information needed for a living thing to grow and develop.

In fact, scientists *have* successfully cloned living things, including plants and vegetables. They have also cloned frogs and mice. Scientists have even cloned a forty-million-year-old bee and a twenty-five-million-year-old termite.

Cloning is a complicated process, and many problems may arise throughout that can stop the growth of a clone. Also, dinosaurs have much more DNA than a bee or an insect. DNA tends to break down over time (and sixty-five million years is a *lot* of time). So even if scientists did find some source for dinosaur DNA, only a very small amount would still exist.

Nevertheless, throughout the course of science, many things have been said to be impossible. Yet over and over again the once unthinkable has been proven possible after all. Could scientists make dinosaurs come alive again?

Only time will tell....

Amber is the hardened sap, called resin, of trees like the pine. Layers of resin build up over time, sometimes catching plant or insect matter in its stickiness. The resin hardens over time until it becomes the hard brownish-gold material called amber.

What really happened to the dinosaurs?

Scientists may never know exactly why dinosaurs became extinct at the end of the Cretaceous Period. But we do know that dinosaurs weren't the only ones to vanish. It's estimated that fifty to sixty-five percent of all plants and animals disappeared. Who survived? Some reptiles (including alligators and turtles), mammals, birds, insects, and fish. Remember this: Correct extinction theory must explain not only why dinosaurs died out, but also why certain animals survived. Here are a few of the most widely held theories (the answer quite possibly involves a combination of all three):

Meteorite Shower/Asteroid Theory

WHAT HAPPENED? A large asteroid hit the earth and sent up a massive cloud of dust and steam that blocked out the sun's rays for weeks or even months. Without the life-giving light of the sun, plants and phytoplankton (tiny ocean animals that are at the base of the food chain) died. With these dead, the larger plant eaters and meat eaters had nothing to eat. They, too, died. Only those animals who could feed off dead animals and plants could live. Thus small scavengers like mammals, crocodiles, and lizards survived.

PROOF Iridium, a rare element found in high percentages in the earth's crust at the end of the Cretaceous Period. This element is found in concentration in the planet's molten core, and is also found in abundance in outer space. (Asteroids contain a lot of iridium.)

PROBLEM? 1) There is no firm evidence of a large crater. 2) The fossils found tend to indicate that the last dinosaurs died thousands of years *before* this layer of iridium was formed.

NEW VERSION Instead of a single asteroid, many large comets hit the earth's surface and caused a series of extinctions over several million years. This also matches the fossil record and explains why there is no large crater.

Colder Climate Theory

WHAT HAPPENED? Paleontologists believe there was a slow cooling of the earth's temperature due to continental drift, which led to many changes in the ocean. This resulted in shifting ocean currents and wind patterns that made the earth even colder. A possible effect is that dinosaurs of only one sex were born (as can happen with crocodiles and turtles today). As a result, the species died out.

PROOF Dinosaur eggs became gradually thinner. This indicates stress caused by difficult conditions. Fossil record indicates that the total number of dinosaur species gradually diminished over a period of eight million years. In essence, the earth changed faster than dinosaurs could evolve.

PROBLEM? This does not fully explain the extinction of marine reptiles. Could gradually cooling water really have killed phytoplankton?

Volcano and Earthquake Theory

WHAT HAPPENED? Due to continental drift, there was a series of violent volcanic eruptions and earthquakes. This produced a cloud of dust and ash around the earth's surface, resulting in a cooling of the earth's temperature.

PROOF Once again, iridium is the main clue. Volcanoes may have blown the iridium from the earth's core. This coincides with the "Meteor Shower/Asteroid Theory," explaining the high concentration of iridium in the earth's crust at the end of the Cretaceous Period.

PROBLEM? Scientists still argue whether volcanic eruptions could really cause such a drastic, long-lasting temperature change of the planet.

ALIENS, anyone?

If our three main theories don't satisfy you, here are a few other (slightly wacky) ideas that have been discussed:

Egg-eating mammals destroyed all the dinosaur eggs.

Disease spread, killing the dinosaurs off.

New, flowering plants caused the dinosaurs to catch hay fever. Ah-choo!

A large star close to the earth exploded, emitting a deadly gas.

Boredom (hey, we're not making this stuff up!).

The dinosaurs "drowned" in their own droppings. Yeech!

And last but not least, our favorite: The dinosaurs were hunted and killed by aliens from outer space!

DINOSAUR RESOURCES

BOOKLIST

All the books in this list have been reviewed by dinosaur paleontologists for scientific accuracy.

All You Need to Know About Dinosaurs
Mark Norell, Sterling, 1991. Gr: 2-9

The Big Beast Book: Dinosaurs and How They Got That Way
Jerry Booth, 1988, Little, Brown & Co. Gr: 3-7

Death From Space: What Killed the Dinosaurs?
Alexander Asimov, Gareth Stevens, 1994, Gareth Stevens, Inc. Gr: 3 & up

Digging Up Dinosaurs
Aliki Brandenberg, 1988, HarperCollins. Gr: pre-3

Digging Up Tyrannosaurus Rex
Don Lesem and John Horner, 1992 Random House. Gr: 2-6

Dinosaurs Are Different
Aliki Brandenberg, 1985, HarperCollins. Gr: pre-3

The Dinosaur Question and Answer Book
Sylvia Funston, 1992, Little, Brown & Co. Gr: 4-7

Dinosaurs Walked Here and Other Stories Fossils Tell
Patricia Lauber, 1987, Macmillan. Gr: 2-4

Dougal Dixon's Dinosaurs
Dougal Dixon, 1993, Boyds Mills. Gr: 3-6

New Questions and Answers About Dinosaurs
Seymour Simon, 1990, Morrow. Gr: 2-5

Raptors!: The Nastiest Dinosaurs
Don Lessem, 1996, Little, Brown & Co. Gr: 3-6

The Search for Dinosaurs
Dougal Dixon, 1996, Steck-Vaughn. Gr: 4-7

Tyrannosaurus Rex and Its Kin: The Mesozoic Monsters
Helen Roney Sattler, 1989, Lothrop. Gr: 3 & up

What Color Is That Dinosaur?
Lowell Dingus, 1994, Millbrook. Gr: 4-6

Where Dinosaurs Still Rule: A Guide to Dinosaur Areas
Debbie Tewell, with Gayle C. Shirley, 1993, Falcon Press. All ages

Where to Look for a Dinosaur
Bernard Most, 1993, HBJ. Gr: pre-3

Most of these books plus games, software, videos, audio cassettes, fossil castings, models, and replicas can be found in The Everything Dinosaur Catalogue, which can be ordered by calling 1-800-346-6366.

DINO MUSEUMS

ALASKA
University of Alaska Museum
Fairbanks, AK (907) 474-7505

ARIZONA
Museum of Northern Arizona
Flagstaff, AZ (602) 774-5211

CALIFORNIA
San Diego Natural History Museum
Summer 1997: "The Dinosaurs of Jurassic Park" exhibit
San Diego, CA (619) 232-3821

California Academy of Science
Golden Gate Park
San Francisco, CA (415) 750-7145

University of California Museum of Paleontology
Berkeley, CA (510) 642-1821

Natural History Museum of Los Angeles County
Los Angeles, CA (213) 744-3466

COLORADO
Denver Museum of Natural History
Denver, CO (303) 322-7009

Devils Canyon Science & Learning Center
Fruita, CO (970) 858-7282

Dinosaur Valley
Grand Junction, CO
(303) 243-3466

CONNECTICUT
Peabody Museum of Natural History
New Haven, CT (203) 432-5050

FLORIDA
Museum of Science and History
Jacksonville, FL (904) 396-7062

GEORGIA
Fernbank Museum
Atlanta, GA (404) 370-0960

ILLINOIS
Field Museum of Natural History
Chicago, IL (312) 922-9410

Fryxell Geology Museum
Augustana, IL (309) 794-8513

Museum of Science and Industry
Chicago, IL (312) 684-1414

INDIANA
Children's Museum of Indianapolis
Indianapolis, IN (317) 924-KIDS

KANSAS
Sternberg Memorial Museum
Fort Hays, KS (913) 628-4286

Museum of Natural History of the University of Kansas
Lawrence, KS (913) 864-4540

LOUISIANA
Audubon Institute Pathways to the Past Museum
New Orleans, LA
(504) 861-2537 (ext. 441)

Museum of Natural Science
Baton Rouge, LA (504) 388-2855

Louisiana Arts & Science Center
Baton Rouge, LA (504) 344-LASC

MASSACHUSETTS
The Museum of Comparative Zoology
Cambridge, MA (617) 495-3045

Museum of Science
Boston, MA (617) 723-2500

Pratt Museum of Natural History
Amherst, MA (413) 542-2165

MICHIGAN
University of Michigan Exhibit Museum
Ann Arbor, MI (313) 764-0478

Cranbrook Institute of Science
Bloomfield Hills, MI
(810) 645-3200

MINNESOTA
The Science Museum of Minnesota
Saint Paul, MN (612) 221-9488

MISSOURI
St. Louis Science Center
St. Louis, MO (314) 289-4400

MONTANA
Museum of the Rockies
Bozeman, MT (406) 994-2251

Old Trail Museum
Choteau, MT (406) 466-5332

Carter County Museum
Ekalaka, MT (406) 775-6886

NEW JERSEY
New Jersey State Museum
Trenton, NJ (609) 292-6308

Princeton Natural History Museum
Princeton, NJ (609) 258-3000

NEW MEXICO
New Mexico Museum of Natural History
Albuquerque, NM
(505) 841-2800

Ruth Hall Museum of Paleontology
Ghost Ranch, Abiquiu, NM
(505) 685-4333

NEW YORK
American Museum of Natural History
New York City (212) 769-5100

The New York State Museum
Albany, NY (518) 474-5877

Buffalo Museum of Science
Buffalo, NY (716) 896-5200

NORTH CAROLINA
State Museum of Natural Sciences
Raleigh, NC (919) 733-7450

NORTH DAKOTA
Dakota Dinosaur Museum
Dickinson, ND (701) 225-DINO

University of North Dakota Leonard Hall Museum
Grand Forks, ND (701) 777-2011

OHIO
Cleveland Museum of Natural History
Cleveland, OH (216) 231-4600

PENNSYLVANIA
Academy of Natural Sciences
Philadelphia, PA (215) 299-1020

Wagner Free Institute
Philadelphia, PA (215) 763-6529

Carnegie Museum of Natural History
Pittsburgh, PA (412) 622-3172

State Museum of Pennsylvania
Harrisburg, PA (717) 787-4978

SOUTH DAKOTA
Black Hills Museum of Natural History
(temporary location)
Hill City, SD (605) 574-4289

Museum of Geology
South Dakota School of Mines & Technology
Rapid City, SD (605) 394-2467

TENNESSEE
Creative Discovery Museum
Chattanooga, TN (615) 756-2738

TEXAS
Houston Museum of Natural Science
Houston, TX (713) 639-4600

Dallas Museum of Natural History
Dallas, TX (214) 421-3466

Fort Worth Museum of Science and History
Fort Worth, TX (817) 732-1631

Shuler Museum, Southern Methodist University
Dallas, TX (214) 768-2760

UTAH
Dinosaur National Monument
near Jensen, UT (800) 477-5558

Utah Field House of Natural History
Vernal, UT (801) 789-4002

College of Eastern Utah Prehistoric Museum
Price, UT (801) 637-5060

Utah Museum of Natural History
Salt Lake City, UT (801) 581-4303

Brigham Young University Earth Sciences Museum
Provo, UT (801) 378-2232

VIRGINIA
Virginia Museum of Natural History
Martinsville, VA (703) 666-8600

WASHINGTON
Pacific Science Center
Seattle, WA (206) 357-2700

WASHINGTON, D.C.
National Museum of Natural History (The Smithsonian)
Washington, DC (202) 357-2700

WISCONSIN
Milwaukee Public Museum
Milwaukee, WI (414) 278-2702

University of Wisconsin Geology Museum
Madison, WI (608) 262-1412

WYOMING
University of Wyoming Geological Museum
Laramie, WY (307) 776-4218

OUTDOOR PARKS & SELF-GUIDED TRAILS

ARIZONA
Petrified Forest National Park
Petrified Forest National Park, AZ (520) 524-6228

CALIFORNIA
San Bernardino County Museum Trackway Field Trips
Redlands, CA (909) 798-8570

COLORADO
Comanche National Grasslands
La Junta, CO (719) 384-2181

Dinosaur Hill
Grand Junction, CO (970) 242-0971

Dinosaur Ridge
Morrison, CO (303) 697-3466

Rabbit Valley Trail Through Time
Grand Junction, CO (970) 244-1480

Riggs Hill
near Grand Junction, CO
(970) 244-1480

Garden Park Paleontological Society
New Cañon City, CO (719) 269-7150

CONNECTICUT
Dinosaur State Park
Rocky Hill, CT (860) 529-5816

NEW MEXICO
Clayton Lake State Park
Clayton, NM (505) 374-8808

SOUTH DAKOTA
Dinosaur Park
Skyline Drive, Rapid City, SD
(605) 343-8687

TEXAS
Dinosaur Valley State Park
Glen Rose, TX (817) 897-4588

UTAH
Cleveland-Lloyd Dinosaur Quarry
Price, UT (801) 636-3600

Mill Canyon Dinosaur Trail
near mile marker 141 on Highway 191
Moab, UT

WEBSITES
Here are some cool dinosaur websites to check out:

Dino Russ's Lair:
http://128.174.172.76/isgsroot/dinos/dinos_home.html

Dinosaur Art and Modeling:
http://www.indyrad.iupui.edu/dinoart.html

Dinosauria On-line:
http://www.dinosauria.com/

The Dinosaur Society:
http://www. dinosociety.org

Paper Dinosaurs:
http://www.lhl.lib.mo.us/pubserv/hos/dino/welcome.htm

The Society of Vertebrate Paleontology:
http://eleweb.lscf.ucsb.edu/svp/

If you want to become a real dino expert, join the Dinosaur Club. You'll get: twelve issues of *Dino Times*, Dino Club stickers, posters, official Dinosaur Society watch, and you can join the DinoMail Dinosaur Club Pen Pal Network to find out what other kids around the world think about dinosaurs. To join, write, fax, call, or e-mail:

The Dinosaur Society
200 Carleton Avenue
East Islip, New York 11730
Tel: (516) 277-7855 or
Toll-Free: (800) 346-6366
Fax: (516) 277-7855
E-Mail: dsociety@aol.com

THE LOST WORLD JURASSIC PARK

JOIN THE OFFICIAL **JURASSIC PARK**™ DINOSAUR CLUB!

1 year membership only $19.95

Send check, money order or VISA/MasterCard information along with name and address to:

Jurassic Park Dinosaur Club
P.O. Box 111000
Aurora, CO 80042

"If we can only step aside, and **trust** in nature, **life** will find a way."

—John Hammond
The Lost World